Where's Whitney?

Written by

Debbie & Michael W. Smith

Illustrated by

Bridget Starr Taylor

Zonderkidz

The Children's Group of Zondervan Publishing House

Where's Whitney?
Copyright © 1999 by Debbie and Michael W. Smith
Text copyright © 1999 by Debbie and Michael W. Smith
Illustrations copyright © 1999 by Bridget Starr Taylor
Requests for information should be addressed to:

Zonderkidz

The Children's Group of ZondervanPublishingHouse
Grand Rapids, Michigan 49530
www.zonderkidz.com

Zonderkidz is a trademark of The Zondervan Corporation

Library of Congress Cataloging-in-Publication Data
Smith, Debbie, 1958–.
    Where's Whitney / written by Debbie and Michael W. Smith : Illustrated by Bridget Starr Taylor.
        p. cm.
    Summary: When she goes with her family to the amusement park Kidsworld, Whitney crawls inside a plastic dragon and gets left behind, causing her family members to pray for her safety when they notice that she is missing.
    ISBN 0-310-20717-7
    [1. Lost children—fiction. 2. Amusement parks—fiction. 3. Christian life—fiction.] I. Smith, Michael W., 1957– II. Taylor, Bridget Starr, 1959– ill. III. Title.
PZ7.S6446835Wh 1999
[E]—dc21 99-10196
                CIP

Art direction and design by Jody Langley

Printed in Hong Kong

99 00 01 02 03 04 05 /v HK/ 10 9 8 7 6 5 4 3 2 1

To the memory of "Boompop," my wonderful grandfather, who
taught me much about life, love, and parenting.
We miss you.
— D.S.

To my sisters, Tamar and Trummy.
— B.S.T.

"Has anyone seen Whitney?"

Dad called from the kitchen.

The Smith family was getting ready to leave for their beach vacation. The luggage was packed, waiting to be loaded. The van was parked in the driveway, full of coloring books, drinks, and snacks for the long trip. The hamster slept peacefully in her cage at the neighbor's house. Everything was ready. Everyone was ready except … **Whitney!**

"I haven't seen her, Dad!" seven-year-old Ryan called from the den.

"I don't know where she is," Mom said, picking up baby Anna from her crib.

"Her not here!" little Tyler said.

Dad searched the house while everyone else got settled in the van. Finally, behind her closed closet door, he found Whitney!

"Sorry, Daddy." She grinned up at him.

"I was just playing with my dolls."

"Okay, Whit," Dad said as patiently as he could.

"But next time you really need to pay attention. You don't want to miss our vacation, do you?"

"No way!" Whitney jumped to her feet.

And in no time, the family was on their way to the beach.

The week in the big vacation house flew by. Cousins, aunts, uncles, and grandparents splashed in the salty waves and built huge sand **castles.**

Whitney loved to pretend she was a princess who lived in the sandy castle. She dreamed of long gowns and carriage rides and knights who slayed terrible **dragons.** Sometimes she didn't even hear her name called for lunch. But that was okay … it was vacation time. The best family vacation ever!

At dinner one evening, Dad made a suggestion.

"How about going to Kidsworld?"

"Yea!" the children shouted.

"I want to ride the ferris wheel!" cousin Jonathan shouted.

"I want to ride the boats!" cousin Jennifer squealed.

"Me ride! Me ride!" Tyler jumped up and down.

"Will they have rides for old folks like me?" Great-grandpa Boompop asked.

Whitney just grinned.

At Kidsworld, the cousins, aunts, uncles, and grandparents piled out of the two vans. The children didn't miss a single thing! The older kids loved the roller coasters and bumper cars. And even the toddlers squealed excitedly on the carousel.

The day passed too quickly, and soon it was time to go. "We need to put the babies to bed," Aunt Pam said.

"Besides," Uncle Mark put in, **"the park will be closing soon."**

But one more thing caught Whitney's eye.

"Dragons!" she cried.

"Where?" Dad asked. He turned to see. Sure enough, two giant plastic dragons watched over the exit gate.

"May we play on them?" Whitney asked.

"Okay, but you'll have to hurry," Mom said. "We need to get back to the house."

The children climbed onto the dragons and jumped inside.

"Roar!"

"I am a brave and fearless knight!"

"Watch out! There's fire coming from his nose!"

Scraping her knees a bit, Whitney crawled deep into the tail of the dragon.

The tail was a perfect fit. Whitney hugged her knees and pretended she was a prisoner in the dragon's cave. She had to be very quiet so she wouldn't waken him. Shh ...

Finally, feeling cramped and achy, she scrambled out from her hiding place. She hopped out of the plastic dragon and looked around.

Where had everyone gone?

Her heart stood still. If only she had paid attention! Now what should she do?

"If you ever get lost," her mother had said,

"look for **someone safe** and ask for help."

Her eyes searched the large parking lot.

Then she saw a mother with two kids. She hurried

over to the woman and tugged on her skirt.

"I'm lost!" she said.

Soon Whitney was safe inside the ticket booth, slurping

a grape slushy while she waited for her mom and dad

to come get her.

Back at the beach house, the babies were changed,
the crab nets were found, and the older cousins and
the uncles headed to the beach.

After a little while, Dad stopped chasing crabs and
squinted into the darkness, counting heads.
"One, two, three …" Wait a minute.
Something was wrong.

"Has anyone seen Whitney?"

"Not me!" said brother Ryan, swinging his crab net
high into the dark sky.
"I haven't seen her," said great-grandpa Boompop,
from his chair on the deck.
"I thought she came back in the other van," Mom said,
rocking Anna in her arms.
"Waaah!" cried baby cousin Joshua.

The family gathered in the kitchen to make a big scary discovery. **They had left Whitney at Kidsworld**! And it was closing time!

"Mom and I will go back to look for her," Dad said, with a worried frown on his face.

"The rest of you stay here and **pray**."

Mom and Dad drove as fast as they dared, praying all the way. "Dear God, please protect our little girl and let her find someone to help her," Mom said.

"But most of all, please don't let her be afraid!"

Finally Mom and Dad pulled into the parking lot at Kidsworld. It was nearly empty, and the lights were blinking off. **Where was Whitney?**

They checked the Ferris wheel. The huge ride looked like a great dark monster against the night sky. They hurried to the plastic dragons, now looking like hungry beasts, their mouths open and snarling. Then they noticed a small group of people standing by the ticket booth. **Could it be ... ?**

Dad ran over to see. There, holding the hand of a man in a Kidsworld uniform, was a small, blond-haired girl.

"**WHITNEY!**" Dad scooped her up in his arms.

Laughing and crying at the same time, Mom held on to them both and buried her face in Whitney's ponytails.

"**I'm sorry, Daddy,**" Whitney cried.

"I wasn't paying attention."

"It's okay, Whit," Dad said, hugging her tight. "It's okay."

Back with the whole family at the beach house,

Whitney got lots of hugs and kisses. Dad told the story

of what had happened. And when everyone had calmed

down, Great-grandpa Boompop prayed.

"**Dear Lord**, you are our

Protector and Strength," he said.

"Thank you for keeping Whitney safe and free from fear."

After the prayer, there was one more thing the family
wanted to know.

"Hey, Whitney," Ryan asked,

"what's that purple stuff on your mouth?"

Whitney didn't say a single word. She just licked

her lips … and grinned.